THIS WALKER BOOK BELONGS TO:

_____

_____

_____

_____

For Jill and Michael

First published 1991 by Walker Books Ltd
87 Vauxhall Walk, London SE11 5HJ

This edition published 1998

4 6 8 10 9 7 5

© 1991 Nick Sharratt

Printed in Hong Kong

British Library Cataloguing in Publication Data
A catalogue record for this book is
available from the British Library.

ISBN 0-7445-6311-9

What Do I Look Like?

Nick Sharratt

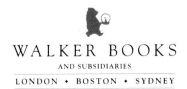

WALKER BOOKS
AND SUBSIDIARIES
LONDON • BOSTON • SYDNEY

What do you look like?

I look like this.

When I'm having fun

I look like this.

When I'm a
scary monster

I look like this.

When I bang
my thumb

I look
like this.

When Cat is a nuisance

When Daddy gives
me ice-cream

When I'm ready for bed

And when I'm fast asleep

I look like this.

MORE WALKER PAPERBACKS
For You to Enjoy

TICKLE MONSTER
by Paul Rogers/Jo Burroughes

If you're ticklish, you'd better watch out – the Tickle Monster's about!
Where is he? Flip the flaps and see!

0-7445-6310-0   £3.99

WHERE'S MY EGG?
by Tony Mitton/Jane Chapman

Hen has lost her egg. Is it in Ben's kennel or Puss's bed or Donkey's straw?
Where can it be? Flip the flaps and see!

0-7445-6312-7   £3.99

WHO'S ON THE FARM?
by Naomi Russell

Who's waiting by the gate? Who's rolling in the mud?
Who's splashing in the stream? Flip the flaps and see!

0-7445-6315-1   £3.99

Walker Paperbacks are available from most booksellers, or by post from B.B.C.S., P.O. Box 941, Hull, North Humberside HU1 3YQ
24 hour telephone credit card line 01482 224626

To order, send: Title, author, ISBN number and price for each book ordered, your full name and address,
cheque or postal order payable to BBCS for the total amount and allow the following for postage and packing:
UK and BFPO: £1.00 for the first book, and 50p for each additional book to a maximum of £3.50.
Overseas and Eire: £2.00 for the first book, £1.00 for the second and 50p for each additional book.

Prices and availability are subject to change without notice.